Goldie Locks
Has Chicken Pox

For Paul and Gianna, with love.
And special thanks to Caitlyn Dlouhy.
—E. D. Z.

To Hiromi, Shota, Aiko, Makoto, and Momoko
—H. W.

Atheneum Books for Young Readers
An imprint of Simon & Schuster Children's Publishing Division
1230 Avenue of the Americas
New York, New York 10020

Text copyright © 2002 by Erin Dealey
Illustrations copyright © 2002 by Hanako Wakiyama

Book design by Edward Miller
The text of this book is set in Imperfect Regular.
The illustrations are rendered in oil paint.
Printed in Hong Kong

2 4 6 8 10 9 7 5 3 1

Library of Congress Cataloging-in-Publication Data
Dealey, Erin.
Goldie Locks has chicken pox / by Erin Dealey ; illustrated by Hanako Wakiyama.—1st ed.
p.   cm.
Summary: When Goldie Locks comes down with chicken pox, she is teased by her brother and is unable to
visit with Bo Peep, Little Red Riding Hood, and other friends.
ISBN 0-689-82981-7
[1. Sick—Fiction. 2. Chicken pox—Fiction. 3. Brothers and sisters—Fiction. 4. Characters in literature—Fiction.
5. Stories in rhyme.] I. Title: Goldie Locks has chicken pox. II. Wakiyama, Hanako, ill. III. Title.
PZ8.3.D3415 Go 2002
[E]—dc21   00-045351

Goldie Locks Has Chicken Pox

by Erin Dealey

illustrated by Hanako Wakiyama

Atheneum Books for Young Readers
New York London Toronto Sydney Singapore

Goldie Locks has chicken pox;
from head to toe were polka dots.

"Where did you get them?" Father said.

But Goldie only shook her head.

Mrs. Locks phoned Mama Bear,
(apologizing for the chair)
but Baby Bear did not have spots
for bears cannot get chicken pox.

"Can chickens get them?"
        Brother yelled,
as Henny Penny rang the bell.
"The sky is falling!!!"
        Henny squawked.
She had no time for
        chicken pox.

"Jack, be nimble! Jack, be quick!
Come and see! My sister's sick!"

But Father told them, "Not today.

When Goldie's better, you can play."

Goldie Locks had chicken pox.

They started out as tiny spots;

then rosy bumps began to form,

and Goldie's temperature was warm.

On her tummy were twenty-four.

On her back, she found twelve more!

All together: thirty-six

small pink dots that itched and itched!

"Please don't scratch them," said her mother.

"Let's connect them!" shouted Brother.

"We might find a teddy bear,
or secret message hidden there!"

"Leave them be," agreed Bo Peep,
who happened by in search of sheep.
"That's sound advice for chicken pox.
It doesn't work for wayward flocks."

"Goldie Locks has chicken pox,
a type of virus," said the doc.
"Give her sodas, ice cream, too;
a nice cool bath will see her through."

"Yum!" said Brother. "I want some!"

The doctor smiled. "Your time will come . . ."

"No fair!" cried Brother, with a pout.

"She gets it all, and I'm left out!"

Little Red came skipping by,

her basket full of cake and pie.

"Can Goldie come to Gram's with me?

I sure would like the company."

But Goldie Locks had chicken pox;
upon her hands she wore her socks!
"Eek—a monster!!" Brother teased,
"oozing polka-dot disease!!!"

"An alien from outer space!"

Her brother laughed and scratched his face.

"I'm SUPER LOCKS. You can't get me!

My powers are too strong, you see!"

"Make him stop!" cried Goldie Locks.

"I can handle chicken pox!

But how am I supposed to rest

when my brother's such a pest?"

Mother warned him, "That will do!"

And then they saw them, then they knew . . .

Her brother's face showed all the signs,
in rosy polka-dot designs . . .